OWL EYES

BY FRIEDA GATES

ILLUSTRATED BY YOSHI MIYAKE

LOTHROP, LEE & SHEPARD BOOKS   NEW YORK

TO JUDIT AND SUSAN —FG

TO ROSAMOND EDISON —YM

AUTHOR'S NOTE

The Mohawk people's own name for themselves is Kanienkehaka (kah-ni-HAH-kah), which means People of the Place of the Flint. *Mohawk* comes from an Algonquian word, *Mohowaug*. The Algonquins and the Mohawks were great enemies, and the term means "eaters of human flesh."

The Kanienkehaka are one of the six nations that make up the Hodinosoni people (how-DEN-oh-see), who through the French became known as the Iroquois Nation because the Algonquins called them *irinaakhoiw,* "real rattlesnakes." The Hodinosoni made their homes in upper New York State.

◆

R AWENO, MASTER OF ALL SPIRITS AND EVERYTHING-MAKER, made the world and everything in it. Before he built the world's high mountains, before he created the wide deserts or the deep seas, he made the woodlands.

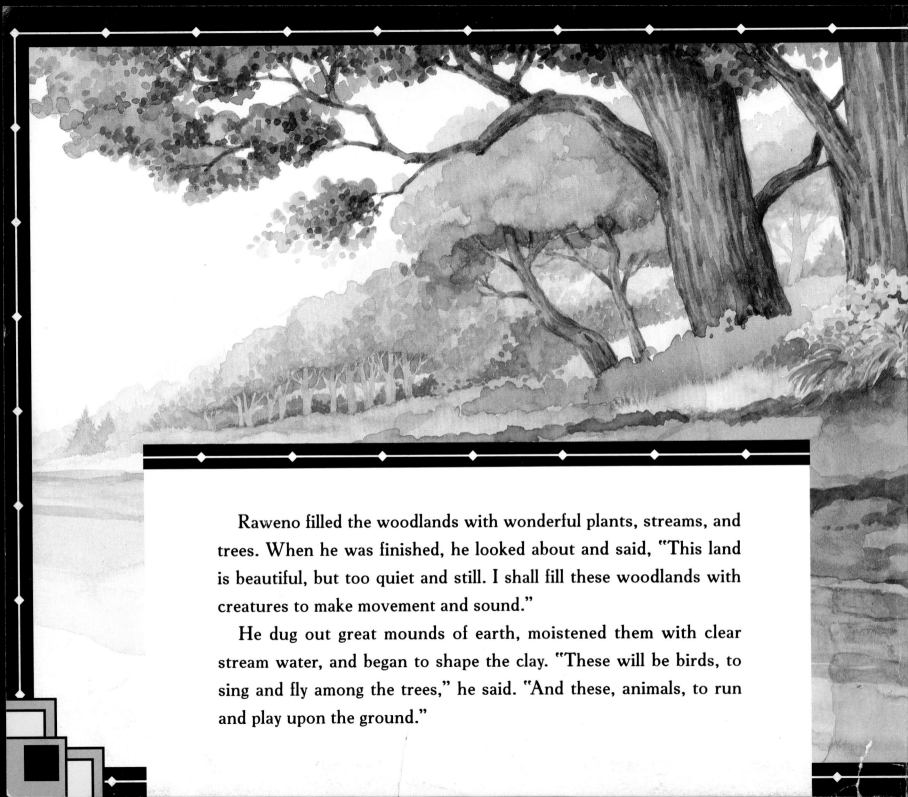

Raweno filled the woodlands with wonderful plants, streams, and trees. When he was finished, he looked about and said, "This land is beautiful, but too quiet and still. I shall fill these woodlands with creatures to make movement and sound."

He dug out great mounds of earth, moistened them with clear stream water, and began to shape the clay. "These will be birds, to sing and fly among the trees," he said. "And these, animals, to run and play upon the ground."

Raweno molded many forms. He gave them small, slitted eyes so they could see, and beaks or muzzles so they could smell and speak. He shaped wings that would someday fly, and feet that would someday run. Raweno gave each of his creatures a name. But he did not finish any of them. He had worked long and hard, and now he wanted to rest.

"I will leave you now," he said, "and while I am gone you will sit and observe the place where you will live. When I return, each of you may choose your colors and however else you wish to be."

A long time passed before Raweno again came to the woodlands, but at last he did return.

Placing Fox on his large, stone worktable, Raweno asked, "How would you like to be?"

Fox was very clear. "I want red fur, a black nose, and a tail that is long and bushy."

Owl, sitting on the ground nearby, called out, "Fox should be yellow like the sun." Raweno ignored him.

Sparrow was a small bird and wished to hide in the shadows, so Raweno began to color him speckled brown. He had finished Sparrow's body and was starting to work on his head when Owl cried, "Raweno, wait! Sparrow's beak is too small." Raweno continued to ignore Owl and went on with his work.

Raweno was fixing Squirrel's jaws, making them large enough to hold nuts, when Owl spoke again: "Squirrel's ears should be longer." Raweno glared at Owl.

Just as Raweno had completed the last of Chipmunk's stripes, Owl called out, "Chipmunk shouldn't have stripes, Raweno. He should be covered with spots."

Raweno scowled. "That Owl is getting on my nerves," he grumbled.

Every time Raweno set to work, Owl had something to say: "Wolf should have smaller feet." "Beaver's tail should be long and skinny." "Mouse should be much bigger."

Finally, Raweno could bear Owl's meddling no longer. He picked up the interfering bird, set him on the worktable, and asked irritably, "How would you like to be?"

Owl answered at once. "I want red feathers like Cardinal's."

Lifting his great hands toward the sky, Raweno was about to cover Owl in red feathers, when Owl suddenly shouted, "No! Not red! Make them blue. Yes, that's what I want. I want blue feathers, just like Blue Jay's."

Raweno glared at the bird and again raised his hands, but again Owl stopped him. "Wait! I don't want blue feathers either. Actually, I don't believe I should have feathers at all. I really should be covered with fur."

"Stop!" growled Raweno, and he grabbed the irritating bird and hurled him onto a branch high up in a tree. "It's obvious that you don't know what you want, so you will sit in this tree until you do."

Raweno turned back to his work and, picking up another unfinished creature, asked gently, "How would you like to be?"

"I'd like a long neck and beautiful white feathers," said Swan.

"I want a long neck too," Owl called from the top of the tree.

"Be quiet!" thundered Raweno, and reaching out one great arm, turned Owl around.

"Now, you troublesome bird," Raweno said, "you will keep quiet, you will face the other way, and you will not watch me while I work!"

But Owl could not keep quiet. He could not stay turned away, and he could not stop watching Raweno work. He twisted and stretched until he was able to see.

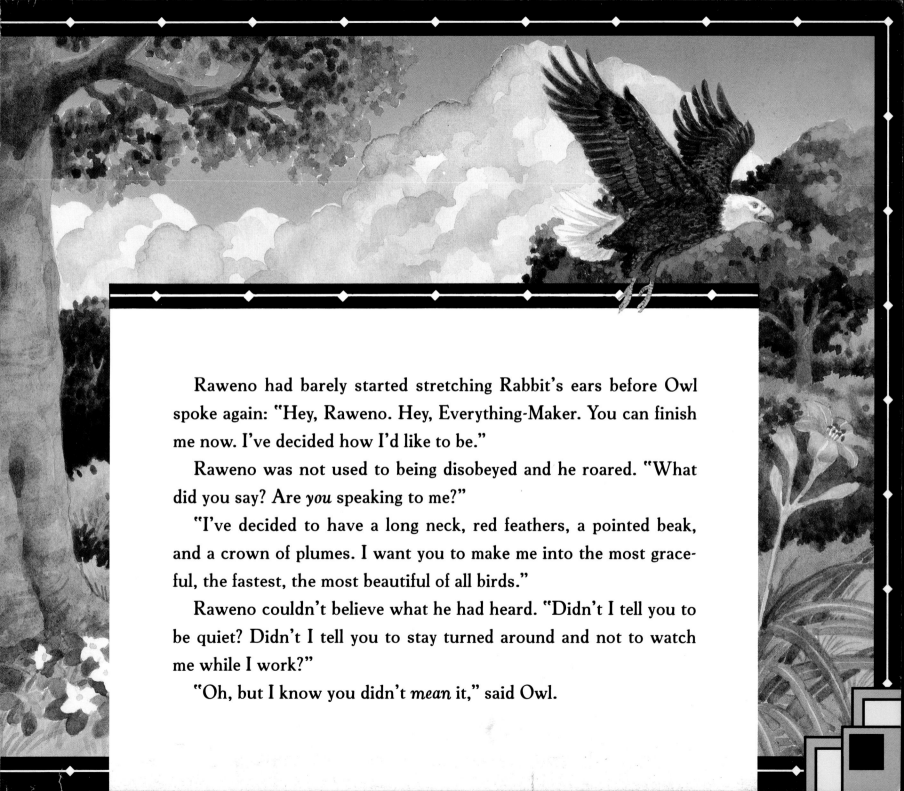

Raweno had barely started stretching Rabbit's ears before Owl spoke again: "Hey, Raweno. Hey, Everything-Maker. You can finish me now. I've decided how I'd like to be."

Raweno was not used to being disobeyed and he roared. "What did you say? Are *you* speaking to me?"

"I've decided to have a long neck, red feathers, a pointed beak, and a crown of plumes. I want you to make me into the most graceful, the fastest, the most beautiful of all birds."

Raweno couldn't believe what he had heard. "Didn't I tell you to be quiet? Didn't I tell you to stay turned around and not to watch me while I work?"

"Oh, but I know you didn't *mean* it," said Owl.

"Such impudence!" said Raweno, and grabbing Owl, threw him onto the worktable. He stuffed the bird's head deep into his body, yanked both ears so they stood straight up, and shook him so hard that Owl's eyes grew large with fright. Finally, Raweno dunked Owl in the mud, coloring his feathers dull brown.

"Now," said Raweno, "your neck is short enough so that you will watch only what is in front of you, and your ears are open enough to hear when you are told what you are not to do. Your eyes are big enough to see in the dark, and your feathers are dull, for you will seldom be seen. And because I work only by day, *you* will be awake only at night."

When Raweno let Owl go, the frightened bird spread his new wings and, hooting, flew far into the distant woodlands.

Now, Raweno could work in peace. He finished all the rest of his woodland creatures, admired his work, and went off to create the rest of the world.

As for Owl, to this day he makes his home deep inside the woodlands, where he sleeps all day, is awake all night, and is seldom seen.